The Dragon with Purple Spots

Tara Kasper

DEDICATION

To My Grandmother

Toby is a happy little green dragon with purple spots and big bright eyes.

Toby lives near a small village.

One day Toby wakes up excited
he runs outside and shouts
"Mommy! Where are you?"

Mommy comes running to Toby.

She recognizes that look in his eyes, "let's play mommy," Toby says while flying two feet above the ground with his little green wings fluttering.

Toby has a best friend whom he loves playing with; it's the Knight who lives in the shiny castle.

"Mommy, will you play with me and Knight today?" his eyes widened while he waits for mommy dragon to reply.

"I would love to play with you, and your friend Toby" she says.

"Let's go to his castle."
Toby and mommy fly all
the way across the valley
to the top of the hill.

They see the big shiny castle, Toby knocks on the big steel Gate and calls out to his friend, but the Knight is nowhere to be seen or heard.

The Guard opened the Gate,
I'm sorry Toby, but the
Knight is not home." I'm not
sure where he went?"

Toby went to the lake by
the village and asked the
people there if they had
seen his friend.

"No Toby we have not seen
the Knight."

Toby then takes flight towards the village and sees the Bladesmith at his shop.

"Have you seen the Knight who lives in the shiny castle?" he asks the bladesmith.

"No Toby, he already bought his swords from me yesterday. I'm not expecting him again for a while.

Toby was starting to get a little worried.

He flew up high and sat on the clock tower while looking around the entire village but he could not see his friend anywhere.

Mommy came flying and said "Cheer up Toby, I'm sure you'll find the knight, but for now look up ahead there's a fair in our town."

"Let's go to the fair that will cheer you up" she said while giving Toby a warm smile.

But, Toby was not in the mood to go to the fair.

The carnival was beautifully lit, there were all sorts of rides, games, and a lot of food.

From the corner of his eye
Toby caught a glimpse of his
friends getting cotton candy.

He was so excited! He ran up
to his friends and said "Hello!"

They were all very happy to
see Toby and asked if they
could join him and his friend,
the Knight!

'The Knight!' Toby remembered. He completely forgot; he was supposed to meet the Knight at the fair. Toby saw the Knight coming his way.

He was finally reunited with his best friend, the Knight.

The end.